SYNAPTAK
A BRIGHT SPARK WHO HOLDS
A TORCH FOR TINI

ENOCH
THIS FOREVER KNIGHT WANTS
BEN FOREVER GONE . . .

FOUR ARMS
NO ONE DARES CALL THIS GUY FOUR EYES!

XLR8
SPEED IS THE AIM OF THIS
ALIEN'S GAME

GREY MATTER
PINT-SIZED BRAINBOX

STINKFLY
THE BAD GUYS WISH HE'D
BUZZ OFF!

CANNONBOLT
HE'S ALWAYS READY TO ROLL

EGMONT
We bring stories to life

Published in Great Britain 2009
by Egmont UK Limited
239 Kensington High Street, London W8 6SA

Ben 10 and all related characters and elements
are trademarks of and © Cartoon Network.
(s09)

Adapted from the animated series by
Barry Hutchison

ISBN 978 1 4052 4673 6

1 3 5 7 9 10 8 6 4 2

A CIP catalogue record for this title is available from
the British Library

Printed and bound in Great Britain by the CPI Group

When 10-year-old Ben Tennyson stumbles upon a mysterious alien device in the woods one summer, little does he realise that his life is set to change - forever.

As soon as the watch-like Omnitrix quite literally gets a grip on him, Ben discovers it gives him the ability to transform into 10 different alien super-beings, each one with awesome powers!

Using the Omnitrix to cause super-powered mischief turns out to be fun, but will Ben learn to use his might to fight for good?

READ ON AND FIND OUT . . .

MEET THE CHARACTERS

BEN TENNYSON
SUPER ALIEN-BUTT KICKER!

GWEN TENNYSON
SHARES BEN'S BIRTHDAY
AND HIS QUICK WIT

GRANDPA MAX
LEADER OF TEAM TENNYSON!

VULKANUS
DINO-ALIEN WITH A BIG
ATTITUDE PROBLEM!

SIXSIX
DEVILISH ALIEN BOUNTY HUNTER

ULTIMOS
THIS CAPE LIKES TO PLAY BY THE RULES

TINI
CAN'T TAKE HER FOUR EYES OFF FOUR ARMS!

CHAPTER ONE

A DAY AT THE MUSEUM

Hundreds of light years away, beyond the edges of our galaxy, a swirling yellow wormhole tore open in space. Silently, a small mining ship floated through it. The vessel glided gracefully through a field of asteroids,

before coming to land on the upper deck of a vast space station.

BOOOOM! A powerful energy blast turned the ship to dust. A second ship – this one armed for war – swooped down towards the space station. As it arced past, a bulky shape shot from within.

The object smashed through the upper deck of the station, sending chunks of metal floating off into the vast reaches of space. Inside, it crashed through three more floors, before finally coming to a stop in a wide, dimly lit corridor.

After a moment, the bulky shape slowly stood up, revealing itself to be a huge, dinosaur-headed alien. He stretched his muscular limbs and creaked his thick neck. That landing had been rough, but he'd had worse.

An electrical blast hit him on the chest as the station's automated security systems launched a counter-attack. It gave him a pleasant tickling feeling, but he didn't have time to enjoy it – his name was Vulkanus, and he had a job to do.

A single punch from his spiked fists reduced the security drones to a pile of high-tech junk. His other hand sliced through a thick, metal door like a knife through butter. Ducking his head, he stepped through the broken doorway and into the room beyond.

It was lit only by a faint pink glow, which was coming from a tall glass canister, a small test tube suspended in the air inside it.

Within the test tube, a chunk of strange liquid metal squirmed. Vulkanus allowed himself a toothy grin. He'd found it. He'd found the Element X!

❈ ❈ ❈

A few minutes later, Vulkanus stepped on to the command deck of his own ship. The

captain's chair swivelled round to face him.
An alien bounty hunter named SixSix leaned
forwards from the shadows.

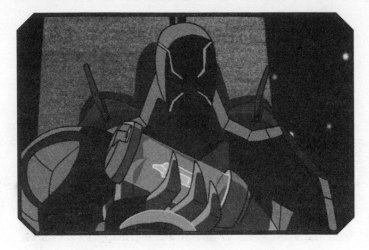

'Element X,' Vulkanus grunted. SixSix
held out a slender, gloved hand. 'It's no good by
itself, you know,' Vulkanus continued. 'Where
are we going to find the bisynthium we need to
make it go boom?'

SixSix touched a hidden button on his
alien armour. A hologram of a blue-and-green
planet suddenly filled the room.

Vulkanus spat in disgust. 'I should have

known. The cesspool of the galaxy.' He scowled. 'Earth!'

Somewhere else completely, a very different threat was stomping along a crowded street, sending terrified citizens fleeing for safety. A gigantic robot towered above the panicked pedestrians, crushing cars beneath its giant metal feet.

Inside the robot's head, a pudgy little man in a ridiculous tight-fitting costume bounced excitedly in his seat.

'Tremble, insects!' he cried. 'Bow and kiss the feet of Lord Doomicus!'

'Oh, yeah?' called a voice from outside.

Doomicus peered down at the street. An all-too-familiar figure stood atop the wreckage of a car, his cape fluttering in the breeze.

'Ultra Ben!' gasped the villain.

Faster than the eye can see, Ultra Ben flew at the robot, his super-strength muscles tensed and ready. The deafening screech of tearing metal filled the air for a moment before Doomicus's robot toppled to the ground, its legs no longer attached.

'My destructoid!' wailed Doomicus. 'Noooo!'

Standing on the remains of one of the robot's feet, Ultra Ben addressed the grateful crowd that had already begun to form around him.

'And any other chump who makes trouble in Tennyson Town is gonna get the same two-fisted justice!' he announced.

The crowd erupted into whoops and cheers. They punched the air as they chanted his name: 'Ultra Ben! Ultra Ben! Ben! Ben!'

'Ben!' cried another voice. Ultra Ben listened carefully. He recognised the voice, but where from?

❈ ❈ ❈

'Ben!' shouted Gwen, snapping her cousin out of his daydream. Perched high on a statue of a giant foot, Ben closed his comic book. Wow, those stories could really suck you in!

'That's a work of art, you know,' Gwen snapped, pointing to the statue he sat on. 'Not your personal butt-rest. You're going to get us kicked out of the museum.'

Ben sighed. If only. 'I don't have that kind

of luck,' he said with a shrug.

'One afternoon of culture won't kill you.'

'Unless it bores me to death,' Ben muttered in reply. He rummaged in his pocket and pulled out a square of chocolate.

'Hey, can I have a piece of that?' asked Gwen.

'Sorry,' said Ben with a smirk, hopping down from the statue. 'Chocolate's for superheroes only.'

'More like super-*jerks*,' said Gwen, walking away in a sulk.

Ben shrugged and headed in the opposite direction. He went out on to the museum steps, hoping the fresh air might help keep him awake.

A shadow passed across him. He looked up to see a battle-ready spaceship drift overhead. Its boosters hissed as it came down for a landing in the middle of the road.

'Maybe this won't be such a boring day

after all,' muttered Ben.

A ring of bystanders had gathered around the ship. They chattered excitedly, amazed by what they were witnessing.

All talking stopped as a door in the ship began to slide open. The onlookers held their breath, waiting to see what would emerge from within the alien craft.

Vulkanus strode down the metal walkway and stared at the humans. He sneered in disgust. How he hated these pathetic creatures.

'Take me to your bisynthium alloy,' he demanded in a voice like thunder. The watching people exchanged puzzled glances. He wanted them to take him to the *what*?

The alien scowled. He was wasting his time. These idiots knew nothing. He would just have to find the stuff himself.

Roaring, he slammed a fist against the ground. The shockwave split the concrete into a web-like pattern of cracks, and sent the humans running for their lives.

Ben ducked behind a building and cranked the dial on the Omnitrix.

'Now that's just plain rude,' he mumbled. 'Someone's got to teach Ugly there some manners!'

At that precise moment, 'Ugly' was raining destruction down on the street. He heaved a car up with one hand, and took aim. The vehicle exploded as it smashed into a second-storey window, showering glass on all those below.

The alien paused when something heavy landed on his back. He craned his neck round

to find a figure with red skin clinging to his shoulders.

'OK, tough guy –' began Four Arms.

'A Tetramand?' Vulkanus growled. 'This planet really *is* a dump.'

With a simple shrug, he launched Four Arms backwards through a shop window, and turned his attention back to the business of destroying everything in sight.

But Four Arms wasn't done yet. Roaring, he burst from within the shop, hitting Vulkanus with an explosive right hook. Caught off guard, the evil alien smashed head first through the wreckage of a car. He lay there, dazed and groaning.

A whirring from the spaceship made Four Arms look up. SixSix erupted through a hatch on the ship's roof, his rocket pack shooting him into the air on twin jets of flame.

Four Arms recognised the alien right away. He'd been one of a pack of bounty hunters who had attacked Ben and his family a few weeks ago. He must have escaped from the space prison he'd been slung into.

SixSix cut loose with a hailstorm of laser gunfire. Four Arms dodged the blasts, then launched himself at his enemy, knocking him from the sky. He caught the villain by his armour and hoisted him high off the ground. That had been almost too easy.

Suddenly, something at his feet began to go **TICK TICK TICK**. Four Arms looked down just as a miniature energy bomb exploded. A crackling surge of electricity curved up from the weapon, cocooning his alien body completely. Four Arms roared and struggled against the powerful bonds, but it was no use. No matter how hard he fought, he couldn't escape them!

CHAPTER TWO

THE GALACTIC ENFORCERS

As Four Arms fought against the agonising energy that wrapped round his body, SixSix took aim with his rockets. He was going to turn this meddling fool into a greasy spot on the pavement.

The bounty hunter tried to launch his weapons, but found himself unable to move. A glowing energy field surrounded his body. It held him motionless for a few seconds, before he found himself hurled through the air. As SixSix bounced on the hard ground, the energy field faded away.

The energy snares around Four Arms vanished with a **FZZZT**. Grateful, but a little puzzled, the alien superhero glanced around to see who had saved him from certain doom.

Three bizarre alien figures stood nearby, dressed in matching yellow uniforms. The alien in the middle – a blue-skinned man with a bald head – stepped forwards, his cape billowing in the breeze.

'No *way!*' grinned Four Arms, realising he had just been saved by some real live alien superheroes!

'OK,' said Gwen as she and Grandpa stepped out from the corner where they'd been

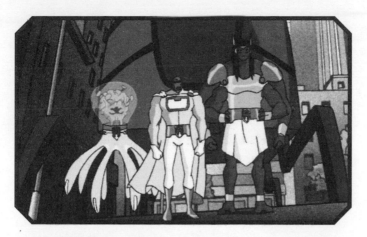

hiding. 'This is weird.'

'Rescue formation Alpha Nine!' boomed the bald blue alien.

Finally freeing himself from the wreckage of the car, Vulkanus glared over at the newcomers and spat. 'It's the Capes,' he spat. 'I *hate* Capes.'

The dino-alien dragged SixSix back to his feet, and together they began attacking with everything they had.

The bald-headed alien leaped into the air, avoiding a spray of laser fire from the bounty hunter. Spinning through the sky, he unleashed a powerful blast of heat vision at SixSix's weapon. The gun quickly turned a blistering shade of red before melting away completely.

The second alien superhero ran forwards. This one looked like Four Arms – a *female* Four Arms! She was the red-skinned alien's exact double, aside from her long black hair and skirt.

Slamming all four of her hands together, she sent a shockwave rippling outwards. The wave caught SixSix, lifted him off the ground, then dumped him back down on his head several metres away.

Four Arms shrank back in horror as his female mirror image turned and winked two of her four eyes at him. A love-struck alien heroine really wasn't a problem Ben needed right now!

A short distance away, the strangest of all the aliens was taking care of Vulkanus. This alien looked for all the world like a floating octopus, except where its head should have been, a giant brain pulsed inside a glass jar.

On the surface of the glass, a computer-generated face pulled itself into a scowl as Vulkanus attacked.

Gliding upwards, the floating brain easily avoided the dino-alien's punches. Using its special powers, it wrapped Vulkanus in another blue energy field before launching him quickly upwards.

As Vulkanus soared into the sky, the bald-headed alien swooped down and delivered him a knockout punch. Vulkanus dropped like a stone back to Earth, landing on top of SixSix with a nasty crunch.

The flying alien gently drifted down until he hovered above the dazed villains. 'By the provisions set forth in The Galactic Code of Conduct,' he announced, 'I order you to surrender. Will you yield?'

'Yield?' Four Arms frowned. 'What is this, a traffic light? Kick their butts before they try to pull something!'

Too late! A compartment in SixSix's chest flipped open, letting a blinking gadget roll free. It exploded in a dazzling flash of white light, blinding the superheroes.

By the time they were able to see, SixSix and Vulkanus were back in their ship. Four Arms braced himself, ready to leap after the fleeing villains.

Before he could make his move, two short laser blasts zapped from the ship's weapon systems. They tore through the twin stone columns of a nearby building. Without the pillars to support it, the entire building began to topple.

Moving quickly, Four Arms ran through the dust and smoke. His mighty muscles bulged as he caught the front of the building and began to push it back up into position.

He felt his arms and legs begin to shake under the strain. They had to go and pick the biggest, heaviest building to knock over, didn't they? Bad guys could be *so* inconsiderate.

The female four-armed alien appeared at his side. She caught hold of the shattered remains of one of the pillars and heaved. Working together, they managed to push the stone columns back up into place.

'You may release your grip now,' said the octopus-like alien, his brain glowing as he spoke. Focusing hard, he held the vast weight in place with the power of his mind long enough for his friend to melt the stone back together with a blast of her heat vision.

Four Arms suddenly felt a strong grip wrap round his neck. The female alien looked him up and down and smiled.

'So,' she breathed, 'what's a big strong alien like you doing on a planet like this?' She leaned in and fluttered all four sets of eyelashes. 'We make a good team, don't we?'

With a **BLEEP**, the Omnitrix began to flash red. Four Arms broke out into a wide grin of relief. '*Yes!*' he cried. 'Saved by the beep!'

One quick transformation later, Ben stood in the alien's place. The female Four Arms frowned at him, puzzled.

'Hey,' she demanded, 'where'd the rest of you go?'

'Sorry, I'm just a kid,' Ben explained, holding up the Omnitrix for her to see. 'I just get some extra hands once in a while.'

'So it is true,' muttered the floating brain, approaching from above. 'The Omnitrix is in the possession of a child. We had heard you were of

a somewhat limited mental capacity.' The alien noticed Ben's expression. 'No offence,' it added quickly.

Gwen and Grandpa hurried over to join the group. 'Don't worry,' said Gwen, smiling. 'He gets that all the time.'

They all turned as the blue-skinned alien came in to land.

'Greetings,' he beamed, 'I am Ultimos, the Specimen Prime. This is Synaptak and Tini,' he continued, pointing towards the floating brain and the female alien in turn. All three of them suddenly struck a dramatic pose. 'We are – The Galactic Enforcers!' announced Ultimos, in a voice that boomed like thunder.

'Whoa! The uniforms, the moves . . . You guys rock!' chattered Ben. 'Finally, some other superheroes I can hang with!'

'As per The Galactic Code of Conduct, we hereby officially request clearance to operate in your quadrant,' said Ultimos.

Ben glanced up at Grandpa, who could only shrug. 'Uh . . . sure,' Ben replied.

Ultimos nodded once. 'Then we have much to discuss,' he said.

Swishing back his cape, the Specimen Prime touched a button on his Galactic Enforcers badge. Three glowing discs of light appeared beneath Ben, Gwen and Grandpa Max.

The light crept upwards until it covered their entire bodies. Ben grinned as he was suddenly launched upwards at an unbelievable rate.

'All *right*!' he cried.

CHAPTER THREE

THE GRAND TOUR

A few hundred kilometres above the surface of the Earth, the sparkling silver headquarters of The Galactic Enforcers drifted silently through space.

On board, three bright lights signalled the arrival of Grandpa, Gwen and Ben. They paused for a moment, waiting for their stomachs to catch up with them. That had been quite a ride!

Grandpa took a deep breath. 'I never did like those transporter discs,' he muttered.

They turned to find Ultimos, Synaptak and Tini standing behind them. The superheroes gestured for them to take a look around.

'How cool is this?' cried Ben as he took it

all in. A large table in the shape of The Galactic Enforcers' logo filled most of the room. On the walls, spare costumes, weapons and high-tech gadgets were suspended by anti-gravity fields. 'I'm in superhero heaven!' he said, beaming.

'Close your mouth, super-dweeb,' said Gwen with a scowl. 'You're drooling all over the place!'

Grandpa, as usual, was straight down to business. 'So,' he asked, 'why did we have the pleasure of Mr Gadget Guy's company again?'

A holographic projection of the alien bounty hunter suddenly appeared beside Ultimos. 'His name is SixSix,' the enforcer explained. 'He escaped incarceration and formed an alliance with the cretin Vulkanus.'

'A Detrabyte,' added Synaptak, bringing up an image of the dino-headed alien. 'Limited mental capabilities. All brawn, no brains.' He looked at Ben. 'You know the type.'

The hologram shimmered. When it took

form again, it showed an image of the test tube
Vulkanus had stolen from the space station.

'They were hired to steal Element X,'
Ultimos continued.

The Tennysons exchanged puzzled
glances. 'OK, we give up.' Ben shrugged.
'What's Element X?'

The hologram changed yet again. This
time it showed a complicated-looking model
of Element X's chemical structure. A model of
another chemical structure – similar, but not
quite the same – hung in the air next to it.

'Element X can be used to form one half of a devastatingly explosive compound,' said Synaptak.

'So, why come to Earth?' asked Ben.

'Most likely in search of the other ingredient,' replied Ultimos. 'Bisynthium alloy. It's very rare, but rumoured to be found on your planet. When combined, the alloy and Element X form an explosive powerful enough to destroy an entire solar system.'

Gwen stared at the hologram. She'd never seen the chemical-structure model of Element X before, but there was something about the second one . . .

'Why does this stuff look so familiar?' She frowned.

'Ah, Gwen,' began Ben, 'I think the giant floating brain guy has it covered.'

'Well, I guess we should get back down there and start looking for them,' said Grandpa Max.

'Excuse me, but The Galactic Code is very clear on our protocol,' announced Ultimos. 'Tini,' he boomed, 'launch Observos one through four!'

Tini crossed to a control panel and pressed a row of buttons. Four miniature satellites launched from below the spacecraft and zipped off towards the distant Earth.

'The Observos will scan every inch of the city and locate the perpetrators,' Ultimos explained. He stepped aside, revealing a shiny metal door. 'In the meantime, perhaps a tour would be in order?'

Max nodded. 'We'd be honoured.'

'Oh, I'm sorry,' said Ultimos, 'but The Galactic Code is quite clear. Provision three seven three dash eight three seven: "No civilian visitors in secure areas of the ship."' He smiled apologetically. 'You and your granddaughter must remain here on the bridge.'

The big blue alien turned to Ben. 'Tini will show you around.'

The female Tetramand yanked Ben off his feet and hoisted him on to her shoulder.

'Hey! How come he gets to go?' demanded Gwen.

Ultimos looked shocked by the question. 'Wearing the Omnitrix grants him *full superhero status*,' he replied. Ben's eyes lit up. Full superhero status. He liked the sound of that!

Synaptak looked on as Tini carried Ben away. For a moment, his digital face seemed to twist into a scowl before he and Ultimos followed Tini off the bridge.

'Don't worry about us. We'll be fine!'
Gwen called after them. When they were safely
out of earshot, she added: 'Super-jerks,' under
her breath.

❄ ❄ ❄

Ben stared out through a huge bay window at
the vastness of space. Stars winked back at him,
brighter than any he'd ever seen before. In the
distance, the planet Mars slowly spun – a fat,
red football orbiting the sun.

'*Whoa!*' Ben whispered. 'That's cool!'

'Ben, here,' Ultimos boomed as he strode
into the room to join the boy and his four-armed
tour guide. 'I want to show you something.'

The alien superhero stopped at a small
table, which had risen from the floor at the
sound of his voice. Ben jumped as an enormous
hardback book landed on it with a **THWACK!**

'This is The Galactic Code of Conduct,'

Ultimos continued. 'Every Galactic Enforcer must learn the rules, so that they may *live* the rules.'

Ben pulled a face. 'Oh, man! Superhero homework?'

'Well, the first twelve thousand pages are a bit dry,' Ultimos admitted, 'but after that –'

A piercing alarm screeched from hidden speakers, halting the superhero mid-sentence. He squared his jaw and clenched his fists. 'The Observos have discovered something!'

✖ ✖ ✖

By the time the superheroes made it back to the bridge, Gwen and Grandpa were already studying a video screen. It showed a rough, rocky terrain. Diggers and other heavy machinery littered the landscape.

Suddenly, two familiar figures appeared from behind a truck. SixSix and Vulkanus skulked towards a mound of rock, unaware their every move was being watched.

'That's a strip mine,' said Grandpa. 'Looks like they're after iron ore. Is that the missing ingredient?'

'We'd better get down there,' said Ultimos, frowning. 'But we could use some help.' He turned to Ben and rested a hand on the boy's shoulder. 'Ben, would you consider a temporary commission in The Galactic Enforcers?'

'Good idea!' Tini grinned.

'*Bad* idea!' Synaptak scowled.

'It seems I am the deciding vote,' said Ultimos. He looked down into Ben's hopeful gaze and quickly made up his mind. 'Let's get you in uniform.'

※ ※ ※

A few short minutes later, the doors to a well-equipped dressing room swished open. A familiar boy in an unfamiliar, oversized costume leaped out, flexing his non-existent muscles.

'Presenting Ultra Ben!' he cried. 'Galactic Enforce—'

Before he could finish, his foot caught on

his cape. Watched by the assembled Galactic Enforcers and his own family, he tripped and landed in an awkward heap.

'I meant to do that,' he groaned.

Grandpa Max turned to Ultimos. 'What about us?' he asked.

'I'm afraid The G.C.C. is quite clear about the participation of non-super-powered beings,' the enforcer replied. 'You'll be safer here.'

Before they could object, an invisible mental shove from Synaptak sent Gwen and Max stumbling back from the transporter.

'Hey!' Gwen snapped. She looked across to her cousin for back-up.

'Sorry, guys.' Ben shrugged, taking a square of chocolate from his pocket and popping it in his mouth. 'This is a superhero thing. We'll be back after we kick SixSix's can.'

Something suddenly occurred to him. Reaching into his pocket, Ben pulled out another piece of chocolate. He held it up to Ultimos. 'Hey, want some?'

'Ah, local cuisine.' Ultimos smiled. 'I certainly wouldn't want to offend your planet's customs.'

He took the chocolate, examined it, then popped it in his mouth. He was still chewing when the flickering light of the transporter engulfed them, whisking them off to Earth.

CHAPTER FOUR

'GALACTIC ENFORCERS, ENGAGE!'

Barely breaking a sweat, Vulkanus poured several tons of iron ore into the back of a flatbed dump truck. Above him hovered SixSix. The bounty hunter held up the canister of Element X and chittered in his strange alien language.

'Once the ore has been purified it can be fused with Element X,' said Vulkanus, his dinosaur-like head pulling into a wicked grin. 'And then – **BOOM!** – the galaxy will be at our feet!'

From behind a nearby tin hut, Ben watched on. 'Now we've got them,' he whispered, turning to the others. 'We'll catch them completely off . . . Ultimos?'

The Galactic Enforcers turned to look at their leader. His bulging, muscular frame was gone. Instead, he stood scrawny and shivering, his blue skin now a deathly shade of grey.

'C-cold,' he trembled. 'So *c-cold.*'

Synaptak hurriedly floated forwards, just in time to catch the falling superhero in his tentacles.

'What's wrong with him?' gasped Ben.

'It appears to be suctratactinite

poisoning,' Synaptak replied. 'But how?' The alien's digital face squinted as he studied Ultimos' mouth. A thin smear of chocolate was just visible on his shrunken lips. 'What is this?' the floating brain demanded.

'I just gave him a little,' said Ben. 'I was just trying to be polite.'

'You did this?' snapped Synaptak. 'I suspected you could not be trusted.'

'Come on,' scoffed Ben. '*Chocolate* is his super-weakness? You have to admit, that's pretty lame!'

'Don't worry, Tini, I have this situation under control,' said Synaptak. He set Ultimos down on the ground and spun towards Ben. 'You'll be dealt with after these rogues are behind bars.'

Before Ben could stop him, the alien brain floated out from behind the hut, and right into the villains' line of sight. 'Galactic Enforcers,' he boomed. 'Engage!'

'What did you do that for?' hissed Ben, as Vulkanus and SixSix readied themselves for combat.

Synaptak scowled. 'As leader, I announced our presence with authority.'

'And let the bad guys know we're here!' added Ben.

The brain's digital face blinked slowly. 'What's your point?'

The two of them were too busy arguing to notice the large shadow passing over them. Luckily, Tini had been paying more attention. She stepped in front, catching a tumbling dump truck before it could crush them.

Synaptak lifted the heavy vehicle with his psychic abilities and launched it back in the direction from which it had come. Vulkanus and SixSix split up to avoid being splattered. The bounty hunter launched himself skyward, while Vulkanus simply dived out of the truck's path.

'By provisions set forth in The Galactic

Code of Conduct, I order you to surrender,'
yelled Synaptak. In response, a rain of laser fire
tore up the ground around him.

'OK, does that *ever* work?!' demanded
Ben as they fled for cover, Tini carrying the
shaking Ultimos over one arm.

'Are you finally going to become a
Tetrimand?' asked Tini, setting Ultimos safely
down behind a rock.

'Not if I can help it,' replied Ben, twirling
the dial of the Omnitrix. They already had brute
strength on the team. What they needed was

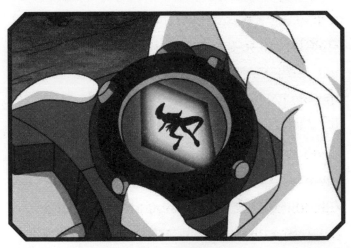

someone a little quicker on their feet.

A cloud of swirling green engulfed him as he activated the watch. In just a few seconds, Ben became the ultra-fast XLR8!

'We've got to split up,' the speedy alien instructed. 'I'll draw their attention and you take out Vulkanus.'

Tini opened her mouth to respond, but a cloud of dust was all that remained where the speedster had stood.

XLR8 rocketed across the quarry floor, dodging SixSix's gunfire easily. Reaching the area directly below the flying bounty hunter, XLR8 began to run in circles. Faster and faster he ran until he was little more than a spinning blur of speed.

SixSix garbled angrily in his alien tongue as XLR8 sent a tornado of sand soaring upwards. The villain was bounced violently around inside the whirlwind before he was eventually thrown free. He hit the ground with a **CRUNCH** and lay still, his head left whirling like a washing machine spin-cycle.

Job done, XLR8 shot off, searching for the other alien menace. A huge chunk of machinery slammed down in front of him, blocking his path. Unable to stop in time, the superhero thudded against the metal and tumbled, winded and dazed, to the ground.

Vulkanus roared in triumph and heaved the machinery above his head. XLR8 looked up, only to see the huge hunk of metal come crashing down towards him!

A split second before XLR8 was turned into an alien pancake, Tini slammed a four-fisted punch into Vulkanus, sending him spiralling away. The machinery bounced over the rough ground and came to a rest several metres away.

'What are you doing?' XLR8 demanded, leaping back to his feet. 'You should be dealing with SixSix!'

'No, I must protect you!' Tini replied.

Recovering quickly, Vulkanus grabbed his chunk of machinery again, this time bringing it crashing down on Tini's head. The impact didn't hurt her, but the thick metal pinned her arms to her sides, making it impossible for her to struggle free.

'Tini!' shrieked Synaptak, rushing over. He hit Vulkanus with a powerful psychic blast, driving the monstrous alien back.

But Vulkanus wasn't the only one to be back in action. A miniature transmitter dish emerged from the arm of SixSix's armour and began sending out a high-frequency pulse. As soon as the beam hit Synaptak, the floating brain dropped like a stone. He was unconscious before he hit the ground.

XLR8 rose up on to the balls of his feet, ready for action. The Galactic Enforcers were down. He was the only one left. This was going to be tough!

✸ ✸ ✸

'They're getting creamed!' cried Gwen, watching events unfold on the space station's video screen. 'We gotta do something!'

Grandpa's fingers glided across the buttons of the station's control panel. 'Already on it,' he nodded. 'I'm programming in the coordinates. We should be beamed right down into the pit.'

Gwen gulped. 'Should?'

Max punched the final button and, before Gwen could object, they were both swallowed by a twinkling haze of light.

✸ ✸ ✸

XLR8 moved faster than even he had ever moved before. Laser fire erupted all around him as Vulkanus wildly lobbed rocks and boulders in his direction. They fell like deadly hailstones, shattering the ground on impact.

Avoiding them wasn't proving too difficult, but the Omnitrix was bound to time out on him before long. If XLR8 didn't take these two jokers down soon, he'd be a sitting duck!

SixSix was the biggest threat, so he needed to be taken care of first. At the moment, he was floating well out of XLR8's reach. Still, that wouldn't prove too much of a problem . . .

Gritting his teeth, XLR8 ran faster still. He zig-zagged past falling stones, then made for the quarry wall. Not slowing, he ran straight up the rocky surface, until he was level with the bounty hunter.

Tensing his legs, he sprang backwards and flipped in the air. His feet quickly kicked out – **BANG! BANG! BANG!** – against SixSix's jaw, and the villain fell back down to Earth once more.

As XLR8 landed, a shimmering blue haze appeared before him. Grandpa and Gwen stepped from the light, both quietly delighted to have arrived in one piece. Whether they could stay that way, though, was a different matter.

Thanks to Vulkanus, a huge chunk of rock was plunging towards them. XLR8 launched himself forwards, knocking his family out of harm's way just before the boulder hit. He lay on top of them, keeping them covered until he was sure the immediate danger had passed.

'Why didn't we stay in that nice, safe spaceship?' Gwen muttered. She looked up as

XLR8 was lit by a bright-red flash.

Ben stared down at his oversized Galactic Enforcers uniform and groaned. Why did this always happen at the worst possible time? He turned to face the villains, but they were already halfway to their ship.

Vulkanus tore the back of the loaded dump truck away from the rest of the vehicle and hauled it on board. They had what they'd come for. The battle, for them, was over. Well, *almost* over . . .

As the ship took off, it unleashed a barrage of laser fire against the high quarry walls. At once, the stones split and began to tumble down the rock face. Within seconds, they had formed a full-scale landslide, dragging more and more boulders down with them as they hurtled towards the helpless superheroes below!

CHAPTER FIVE

THROWING AWAY THE RULE BOOK

Ben glanced down at the fallen Galactic Enforcers and realised there was only one thing to do. Racing forward, he stood before the tumbling mass of rocks, his hands on his hips.

'This is a job for Ultra Ben!' he cried. 'Only I can save Tini!'

On hearing Ben's words, Synaptak summoned up reserves of strength he didn't even know he had. If anyone was going to protect Tini, it would be him!

'Step to one side, Earthling,' he instructed. A psychic shockwave radiated from him, meeting the oncoming landslide. As the two collided, the rocks were reduced to a harmless pile of pebbles and sand.

Drained, Synaptak sunk back down to the ground. From inside her metal prison, Tini gave him a grateful smile.

'You can annoy anyone into action,' whispered Gwen to her cousin.

'It's a gift,' Ben replied.

'We've lost SixSix and Vulkanus,' fretted Grandpa Max.

'The bisynthium alloy and Element X can only be bound together with an enormous amount of heat,' wheezed Synaptak.

'Like the forge of a steel mill?' suggested Max, dreading the answer.

'Are there any such facilities in this area?' asked Synaptak.

'*Hello!*' cried Gwen. 'We're in Pittsburgh! Steel town USA!'

Ultimos staggered from behind a rock. He looked almost back to normal, but he was limping as he joined the rest of the team.

'Interesting theory,' he croaked, 'but according to protocol in The Galactic Code of –'

'Forget protocol,' Ben snapped. 'This time we do it the *Tennyson way*!'

❈ ❈ ❈

In the fiery heart of the closest steel mill, Vulkanus was hard at work. His hands were plunged into a deep container of molten metal as he busily prepared the stolen iron ore.

The hulking monster sighed as SixSix began to chatter excitedly. 'Don't blow a gasket, partner,' he warned. 'Only the purest mixture will combine with Element X to give us the explosive we want!'

The glass canister of Element X clutched tightly in his grip, SixSix nodded. Any minute now it would be ready and they would have everything they needed to rule the galaxy!

Vulkanus took his hands from the melting pot. The liquid metal covering them glowed white hot. He barely felt it.

'Perfect!' He smiled. Nothing could stop them now!

A grinding of metal from above made the villains look up. Synaptak floated down through a hole in the roof, Tini and Ultimos by his side. SixSix took aim with his arm blaster. This would be like shooting fish in a barrel.

Vulkanus sneered. 'You Capes never learn!'

'Wrong!' boomed a voice from behind. A huge, spinning ball spun up from the shadows of the steel plant. It rotated in the air, before slamming into SixSix, sending the bounty hunter sprawling.

'Galactic Enforcers Formation: Surprise Party!' cried Cannonbolt, the largest of Ben's aliens.

'Galactic Enforcers, engage!' yelled Ultimos, and all four superheroes swung into action.

�֍ ✖ ✖

Up in the control room of the steel plant, Gwen and Grandpa pulled levers and fiddled with switches.

'Making steel's like baking a cake,' said Gwen. 'Mess up the recipe and Element X won't bond to it.'

Grandpa nodded. Through the window

above the controls he could see SixSix unleashing a stream of firepower in Cannonbolt's direction. He yanked another lever. They had to act fast.

✹ ✹ ✹

Lasers, missiles and cluster bombs screeched towards Cannonbolt as SixSix attacked with everything he had. The spinning alien ball bounced and rolled, only just managing to avoid the explosives.

Cannonbolt propelled himself towards the bounty hunter. His fire power used up, SixSix lashed out with a laser whip. It caught Cannonbolt by surprise, sending him tumbling towards a vat of molten iron ore.

Just before the superhero sank down into the glowing hot liquid metal, a bubble of psychic energy wrapped round him. Synaptak gave him a brief nod as he set him safely down on the floor. Cannonbolt nodded back. Maybe Synaptak wasn't *too* much of a jerk after all . . .

Up above them, Ultimos and Tini darted along a metal walkway. Ultimos grinned broadly as they ran. 'This is exhilarating, isn't it?' He beamed. 'No plans! No rules! No –'

Tini slammed her shoulder against him, and both superheroes crunched into the wall. A flaming blob of molten metal tore past them, destroying the walkway.

KA-BOOM! The metal punched a hole straight through the control-room window. Gwen and Grandpa leaped back from the scorching console. They looked down at the ruined control panel. There was no way of messing with the mixture now!

Back out among the furnaces, Vulkanus popped the top off the canister containing the glowing Element X. He held it out, dangling it above the purified iron ore, which swirled in the mixing pot below.

A ground-slam from Tini caused the

whole building to shake. At once, the Element X tumbled from Vulkanus's grip.

Spinning fast, Cannonbolt launched himself towards the falling canister. Catching it just before it broke the surface of the liquid metal, his fingers began to sizzle.

'Hothothothothot!' He grimaced, bouncing the canister from one hand to the other. He didn't have time to tend to his wounds though. Vulkanus and SixSix were already closing in on him, determined to get their explosive back.

Unnoticed by the villains, a large pot of

molten-hot metal floated above their heads. Synaptak lowered it and gave it a quick psychic nudge.

A waterfall of blisteringly hot liquid crashed over them, stopping them in their tracks. Ultimos quickly blasted the molten iron ore with a lungful of ice-cold super-breath. Immediately, the metal hardened, trapping Vulkanus and SixSix.

Cannonbolt rolled up and stood by The Galactic Enforcers, admiring the makeshift prison holding the villains in place. 'I don't know if it's art,' he said, grinning, 'but I like it!'

�֎ ✖ ✖

When Vulkanus and SixSix had been safely beamed to a holding chamber on The Enforcers' space station, Ben shuffled up to Tini.

'Uh . . . about that Tetramand thing.' He winced.

'I have found a new partner,' said Tini, smiling. Synaptak floated up behind her and rested a tentacle on her shoulder.

'Ben, your unorthodox methods are exactly what we need to tackle this new breed of criminal,' said Ultimos, handing Ben a badge. 'We officially extend to you a full commission in The Galactic Enforcers.'

Ben glanced at it, then back at his grandpa and cousin. 'Thanks,' he said, 'but no, thanks. I'm already part of a super-team.'

'Keep it,' said Ultimos with a smile, 'in the hope that we meet again someday.' A blue light surrounded the three superheroes. 'Galactic Enforcers, away!' And with that they were gone.

Gwen stepped closer to her cousin. 'You really mean all that stuff you said to Ultimos about already being part of a super-team?' she asked.

Ben turned to face her. 'Nah!' he said, breaking into a grin. 'But who wants to hang with a pack of wackos like that? I'm better off with you guys!'

VULKANUS WON'T LET ANYTHING STAND BETWEEN HIM AND ELEMENT X

AND SIXSIX GETS TO WORK HELPING HIM FIND THE INGREDIENT TO MAKE IT GO BOOM!

AFTER AN ALIEN SHOWDOWN, THE GALACTIC
ENFORCERS BEAM THE TENNYSONS TO THEIR SHIP

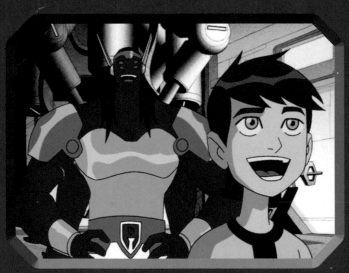

TINI TAKES BEN ON A SUPERHEROES-ONLY
GUIDED TOUR

WHEN THE EVIL BOUNTY HUNTERS MAKE A
COMEBACK, SYNAPTAK TAKES A BLOW.

BUT HE RALLIES ROUND TO PROTECT
HIS BELOVED TINI!

CANNONBOLT SCUPPERS VULKANUS' EXPLOSIVE
PLAN TO RULE THE GALAXY

AND ULTIMOS REWARDS BEN WITH HIS VERY OWN
GALACTIC ENFORCERS MEMBERSHIP!

THE MASK OF AH PUCH IS THE KEY TO THE
POWERFUL SWORD OF EK CHUAH

BEN USES HIS GREY MATTER TO STOP IT FALLING
INTO THE WRONG HANDS

BUT THE FOREVER KNIGHTS HAVE OTHER IDEAS

THE TENNYSONS STAKE OUT THE
TEMPLE OF EK CHUAH

WHEN THEY'RE THROWN INTO THE PIT
OF DESPAIR, BEN GOES ALIEN

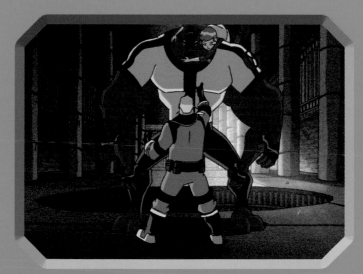

AND FOUR ARMS COMES TO THE RESCUE!

THE SWORD OF EK CHUAH MUST BE KEPT FROM
THE FOREVER KNIGHTS' CLUTCHES

BUT IT CRUMBLES AWAY, AND THE KNIGHTS ARE
LEFT TRAPPED WITH ITS FEARSOME GUARDIAN!

CHAPTER ONE

THE MASK OF AH PUCH

DRRRRRRRR! A tall, powerful drill cut through the dry, dusty earth of a Texas oil field, searching for some more of the gloopy black liquid. Three men stood by it, operating the controls, the sweltering sun almost melting them in their heavy protective overalls.

EEEEEEEEEK! Suddenly, the drill let out an ear-shattering squeal. The men stepped back as hot smoke began to billow up from the hole in the ground. Something was wrong.

The ground at their feet began to move. Small cracks – barely larger than spiders – appeared in the rocky soil. They grew quickly, spreading out in all directions, churning the ground into rubble. Something was *definitely* wrong!

The oil rig workers ran, leaping hurriedly over the cracks appearing before them, trying to get to safety. Huge swirling clouds of dust and sand whipped at them as they fled.

At last, with a deafening **CREEEAK** of metal, the enormous drill toppled down into the gaping hole that had opened up below it. It clanked noisily as it sank down into the darkness, and then a spooky silence fell over the area.

It didn't last long. As the workers crept up

to the edge of the hole for a closer look, a pillar of flame exploded from within it. The column of fire stretched up to the sky, punching clean through the clouds.

The workers watched on, numb with shock as the flames flickered and danced. For a moment, they could have sworn the fire twisted to form an ugly, terrifying face.

Then, a final rush of wind snuffed the fire out as quickly as it had started. In the silence that followed, everyone heard the faint **PLOP** of something hitting the ground. They stepped closer to the fallen object and stared. It stared back.

A mask – its features frozen in an evil scowl – lay on the rock. For a second, its eyes glowed an eerie shade of green.

The drill had struck *something* – but it definitely wasn't oil!

At The Rust Bucket's small dining table, Ben and
Gwen munched on a sample of Grandpa's latest
recipe. It tasted . . . OK. Better than his usual
stuff, anyway. Grandpa himself had already
finished one bowl and was now well into his
second helping.

'Well,' he asked them, 'what do you think?'

The cousins glanced down at their bowls.
It was still too early to give their final verdict.

'What's the crunchy stuff?' asked Ben.

'Dung beetles,' replied his grandfather.

Ben and Gwen spat the food back into

their bowls and hurriedly scraped their tongues with their fingernails. Why couldn't they just have a *normal* meal for once? Would it kill Grandpa to cook a burger?

'What?' the old man asked, smirking. 'Too spicy?' He watched them retching in disgust. 'You'll get used to it.'

A piercing alarm screeched from The Rust Bucket's hidden speakers, startling everyone to attention. Above Grandpa's head, a flat-screen monitor unfolded from a concealed compartment and lowered itself down.

Grandpa Max's face went pale as his eyes fixed on the screen. He leaned closer to the object on the monitor and stared.

It stared back.

'No!' he gasped, his eyes fixed on the glowing green eyes of an all-too-familiar mask.

Gwen and Ben exchanged a worried glance. They'd never seen Grandpa look so scared before.

'Grandpa,' asked Ben. 'What is it?'

'The Mask of Ah Puch,' he replied gravely. He turned the screen so his grandchildren could see for themselves. 'It's the key to the most powerful and destructive weapon ever created.'

Pushing the monitor away, Grandpa Max left the table and slid into the driving seat. Ben scrambled to take his place up front as The Rust Bucket spluttered into life.

'The Mask of Ah Puch is the key to the Sword of Ek Chuah,' Grandpa explained, powering the motorhome along a narrow dusty track. 'The Plumbers searched for it for decades without any luck.'

'Ek Chuah?' Ben frowned. 'What kind of alien is that?'

The windscreen of The Rust Bucket shimmered for a moment before a holographic projection of a map swam into focus. A red light appeared on it, blinking, pinpointing the location of the mask.

'Not alien, *Mayan*,' Grandpa corrected. 'Ek Chuah was the Mayan God of War. His sword was rumoured to have levelled whole cities with just one swipe.'

'Ha! Sounds like just the kind of thing the world's most powerful ten-year-old should have,' said Ben, smirking.

'This is no toy, Benjamin,' his grandfather snapped. The tone of his voice made Ben and Gwen jump in their seats. 'Whoever controls the sword controls the destiny of mankind, and I will *not* let it fall into the wrong hands!'

※ ※ ※

Half an hour later, The Rust Bucket pulled into the oil field. It crept up to the main office building, where the tracking device told Grandpa the mask was being kept.

Watched closely by suspicious security guards, Grandpa Max cut the engine and joined his grandchildren in the back of the motorhome.

'Bet they're keeping it in the basement,' he mumbled to himself. 'Ben, you go alien and sneak in, then open the side door for us.'

'"Sneak in"? Don't you mean *break* in?' suggested Ben.

Grandpa fixed him with an icy glare. 'I haven't the time to explain how important it is for us to get the mask,' he said. 'Now, can I count on you or not?'

'You know you can, Grandpa.' Ben nodded, a little hurt by the way his grandfather was speaking to him.

Without a word, Grandpa Max nodded back, and went to wait up front.

'What's up with Grandpa?' Ben whispered to his cousin. 'He's so . . . *intense.*'

'Cut him some slack, will you?' Gwen replied. 'He's trying to save the world!'

Ben adjusted the dial on the face of the Omnitrix. Saving the world was his speciality!

He slammed his hand down on the watch. Immediately, the cloud of swirling green wrapped round him, altering his DNA.

Ben's pinkish skin grew grey as stone as his entire body began to shrink. His eyes grew bulgy, until they stuck out from his head like two blinking green bubbles. When it came to sneaking into places, not many of his aliens could beat the tiny Grey Matter!

Gwen opened the door of The Rust Bucket just wide enough for him to slip out. After a quick check to make sure the coast was clear,

Grey Matter hopped down from the motorhome and scampered up a drainpipe fixed to the office-building wall.

Inside The Rust Bucket, Gwen and Grandpa watched him go.

'I know Ben can be a major doofus,' Gwen said. 'But don't you think you were a little –'

'You're just kids,' interrupted Grandpa. 'I don't expect you to understand.'

Gwen bit her bottom lip and looked away. Ben was right – their grandfather had *never* acted like this before.

❈ ❈ ❈

On the bathroom floor of the office building, a round metal drain cover rose a few centimetres into the air. With a grunt, Grey Matter pushed his way through, before letting the cover slip back over the hole.

The little alien groaned when he realised

a large blob of chewing gum had got stuck to his head somewhere along his journey.

'Oh, man,' he complained, 'I should've just gone Cannonbolt and *busted* my way in!'

He flicked the chewing gum away, then stopped. A warm breeze had suddenly begun to blow against the back of his neck. If he listened closely, he could also make out a slow, regular wheezing. It sounded almost exactly like . . . *breathing*!

Grey Matter spun round, then gulped down a mouthful of panic. A German Shepherd dog loomed over him, its gums pulled back to expose two rows of sharp, yellowing teeth.

He backed away, only to hear a growling from the other direction. Turning, his worst fears were confirmed. There were two of the dogs – and they were coming right for him!

CHAPTER TWO

THE FOREVER KNIGHTS

As the dogs leaped, so did Grey Matter. The alien sprang upwards on his frog-like legs, just as the two crazed canines pounced. Both dogs gave a yelp of pain when their heads knocked together with a hollow **THWOCK!**

Grey Matter scurried for the bathroom door, rushing to get away before the stunned mutts came back to their senses. As he scampered through the door, he hurried back out and heaved it closed behind him, trapping the animals inside.

'Ha!' the alien cried, listening to their frenzied barking. 'Who's the big dog now?'

By the side wall of the office building, away from the prying eyes of the security guards, Grandpa Max impatiently tapped his foot. There was a narrow hatchway here, leading down into the building's basement area. Ben should have opened it up by now. What was keeping the boy?

The door handle gave a **CLUNK** and swung open. Grey Matter hopped out, ready to be congratulated on a job well done.

'About time,' Grandpa muttered. Grey Matter watched sadly as Grandpa Max trudged on down the stairs, not saying another word.

Gwen reached down and picked the tiny alien up by the back of his shirt. She sniffed him cautiously before screwing up her face in disgust.

'Ewww!' she winced. 'Why do you smell like dog slobber?'

Carrying Grey Matter on her shoulder, Gwen descended the steps behind her grandfather, being careful to leave the door unlocked behind her.

✖ ✖ ✖

Up above, unnoticed by any of the Tennysons, a black car with darkened windows drew up next to The Rust Bucket.

✖ ✖ ✖

Grandpa Max marched along the basement corridor, searching for any sign of the mask. Behind him, Gwen raced to keep up, Grey Matter holding on to her ear for dear life.

'Have you ever seen Grandpa this serious?' Gwen whispered.

Grey Matter shook his head. 'I've never seen *anyone* this serious!'

Grandpa threw open a door and stepped into a small office. A desk and chair stood in one corner. Next to them was a large, cast-iron safe.

'It *has* to be in here,' he said.

'I'm on it!' cried Grey Matter. The super-genius alien hopped on to the safe and pressed his ear against the solid door. With one foot, he twirled the dial of the locking mechanism, listening for the clicks that would tell him the lock pins were falling into place.

In just a few seconds, the door swung open.

'Good job, Ben!' said Gwen.

Grandpa didn't speak. Instead, he pulled the door fully open. A faint gasp escaped his lips as his eyes fell on the contents of the safe.

'Beautiful, isn't it?' he said. Gwen and Grey Matter peered in at the hideous mask.

'Ah, not exactly . . .' shrugged the little grey alien.

Grandpa Max picked up the mask, his hands trembling. He stared into the empty eye sockets, as if hypnotised by them.

'Over forty years of searching,' he mumbled, 'and now, finally, you're –'

'I thought you'd retired from the plumbing business, Mr Tennyson,' boomed a voice from behind the group. They turned to find three men blocking the doorway, their faces obscured by expressionless metal masks. The lead man stepped forward. 'Or may I call you Max?'

Grey Matter's eyes narrowed. They'd encountered these guys already during the summer. They were bad news.

'It's Enoch and those Forever Knight guys who tried to slice and dice me!' he hissed.

'How nice of you to remember,' spat Enoch. 'And, of course, how can I forget the family who left the Forever Knights without a castle?'

'Whatever happened you brought upon yourselves,' scowled Grandpa Max.

'Aren't we the feisty sewer rat?' drawled Enoch. 'I'd love to chat about old times, but I'm late for holding the world at my mercy, so I'll be taking that mask now.'

Grandpa Max narrowed his eyes. 'Over my dead body.'

'Excellent suggestion,' chuckled Enoch. He gestured to his two henchmen. 'Gentlemen . . .'

In unison, the two masked villains drew their swords. The blades cracked and crackled with an electric-blue glow.

'Hey, what's going on here?' A security guard blundered through the door behind the Forever Knights, completely unaware of what he was about to get himself into.

Taking advantage of the distraction, Grey Matter sprang at Enoch, draping himself over the villain's eyes like a blindfold.

'Run!' he shouted, clinging on tightly.

Grandpa and Gwen didn't need telling twice. The Mask of Ah Puch clasped tightly under Grandpa Max's arm, they dodged past the knights and shoulder-barged the security guard out into the hallway.

'We've got burglars,' yelled the guard into his walkie-talkie. 'Seal the exits!'

Enoch roared and tore the squirming Grey Matter off his mask. With a flick of his wrist, he sent the alien spinning across the room before the three knights set off in pursuit of Grandpa and Gwen.

Grey Matter hit the top of the desk and skidded across its surface, sliding closer and closer to the edge. As his feet slipped off the desktop, the bug-eyed alien twisted and threw out his arms. His stick-like hands caught hold of a bundle of papers. His body slammed hard against the side of the table – **THUNK!** – but still he hung on.

Below him lay the sharp metal jaws of a paper shredder. If he fell on to them, they'd whir into life, chopping him into hundreds of little squidgy bits.

'No way I'm winding up as alien

coleslaw!' he said, pressing his feet against the side of the desk. With a heave, he launched himself backwards, flipped twice in the air, then landed safely on the office floor. Grey Matter allowed himself a brief smile. If he ever gave up crime-fighting, he could always start a career as a gymnast!

✶ ✶ ✶

Grandpa rushed up a flight of metal stairs, taking them two at a time. Gwen hurried along behind. For an old man, her grandfather sure could move when he wanted to!

At the top of the stairs, Grandpa Max pulled back. Two security guards stood by the exit, their backs to the Tennysons.

'Wrong way,' Grandpa hissed, changing direction. He led Gwen towards a set of wide double doors, which he hoped would lead them outside.

Suddenly, Grandpa felt the mask slip from his grasp. He whipped round, clawing at the air, desperately trying to catch it. It was no use. A high-tech grappling hook had snared the mask, and was pulling it back to the waiting Enoch.

'Your loss is my gain,' sneered the knight as he and his two companions turned and fled.

A shadow began to fall across Grandpa and Gwen. They turned to see a thick metal shutter lowering down in front of the door. If they didn't move fast, they'd be trapped!

'Grab on,' Grandpa barked, catching Gwen by the hand. Side by side, they sprinted for the exit. The shutter was almost fully closed. This was going to be a tight squeeze!

Throwing themselves to the floor, Grandpa Max and Gwen slid beneath the steel shutter. The sharp metal bottom brushed against Grandpa's bulging belly, but they made it through just before it clanged fully closed.

Outside, a grey shape dropped from the mouth of a drainage pipe. It screamed and flapped its arms as it plummeted down into a dumpster full of rotting garbage.

In a bright flash of red, a full-sized Ben found himself sitting among the rubbish. Flies buzzed around him, and crawled across a mouldy banana skin balanced on his head like a particularly smelly hat.

Ben grimaced. 'I hate it when this happens.'

The Rust Bucket's brakes squealed to a stop just in front of him. 'We don't have time to fool around, Ben,' Grandpa bellowed. 'Get in!'

Ben clambered free of the mound of garbage and jumped into The Rust Bucket. Even before the door was closed, Grandpa slammed the vehicle into reverse and screeched out of the car park. The Forever

Knights had the Mask of Ah Puch, *and* they had a head start. If they weren't caught, they could find the Sword of Ek Chuah, and then the world would be theirs for the taking!

CHAPTER THREE

HIGH-SPEED PURSUIT

A sleek, black sedan car sped along a Texan track, spraying up clouds of dust in its wake. In the back seat, Enoch studied the Mask of Ah Puch, all the while laughing the laugh of a madman. He had found the mask. Soon all the power in the world would be his!

Up in front, one of Enoch's two guards glanced in the rear-view mirror. His eyes narrowed behind his mask as he tried to make out the shape of the large object tearing along the track behind them. His hands tightened on the wheel when he realised The Rust Bucket was closing on them fast.

But not fast enough for Grandpa Max.

Flicking a switch on the dashboard, he activated the motorhome's turbo mode. The hidden jet engines clicked into place, and a powerful blast of flame sent the vehicle rocketing along the road.

CLANG! The front of The Rust Bucket slammed hard against the back of the Forever Knights' car. Inside, Enoch was bounced around wildly in his leather seat.

The masked villain's fingers flew to a control panel mounted into the back of the seat in front. At the touch of a screen, the boot of the car sprang open and a spinning saw blade lashed out, cutting a deep scar into the front of The Rust Bucket. Grandpa was forced to pull back before the blade cut clean through the motorhome's engine.

'Come on,' cried Gwen, giving her cousin a nudge. 'Wildmutt? Ripjaws? *Somebody?*'

Ben frantically spun the dial on the Omnitrix. It glowed red – not yet recharged enough to spring back into life.

'I'm trying,' Ben protested, 'but the stupid watch won't let me!'

In the driver's seat, Grandpa Max reached a decision. 'This is a job for a Plumber,' he announced, before pushing a button on the steering wheel.

'Auto-driver engaged,' stated a computer voice from somewhere behind the dashboard.

Without a word, Grandpa swivelled in his chair, walked to the back of The Rust Bucket, and locked himself in the toilet. Ben and Gwen stared at the door to the small wooden cubicle in stunned silence.

At last, Ben gave a shrug. 'Well,' he said, 'I guess when you gotta go, you gotta go.'

�֍ ✖ ✖

In the car in front, Enoch had turned his attention back to the Mask of Ah Puch. He turned it over in his hands, letting the light streaming in through the sunroof catch the mask's emerald-green eyes. As the sun's rays struck them, they became twin beams of power. Enoch watched the beams combine to form something wondrous.

'Excellent!' he crowed, his own eyes sparkling like stars beneath his metal faceplate. The mask worked, just as the legends had said! It had told him where to find the sword. There would be no stopping him now!

※ ※ ※

The door to The Rust Bucket's tiny toilet flew open. Grandpa stepped from inside, no longer wearing his familiar orange Hawaiian shirt. Instead, he was kitted out in the grey boiler suit and body armour of a Plumber.

'Uh, Grandpa . . .' Ben frowned. 'What's with the fashion show?'

'It's my Plumber suit,' his grandfather replied. 'Been saving it for the right time.' He glanced through the side window. The Forever Knights' car was right alongside them. 'Like now,' he finished.

Taking two magnetic pads from his belt and slipping them over his hands, Grandpa pulled open the door of the motorhome. He calculated the distance between the two vehicles carefully. The suit was tight and he wasn't as fit as he'd been last time he wore it, but he was still fairly sure he could make the jump.

With a grunt of effort, Grandpa Max hurled himself on to the top of the knights' car. He skidded across the roof, looking certain to slide off the other side. At the last moment, he slammed the magnetic pads down on to the roof. They stuck fast to the metal, holding him in place.

Gritting his teeth, Grandpa crawled across the roof of the long car, towards the open sunroof. He was so fixated on getting the mask back, he didn't notice the two eerie figures standing on top of The Rust Bucket. The Forever Knights cracked their knuckles menacingly. The Plumbers weren't the only ones to have auto-driver mode on their vehicles!

Grandpa edged closer to the sunroof and peered inside. There was the mask, sitting by itself on a seat! He gave a sigh of relief. This must be his lucky day!

SSSSSHCK! A shimmering blue blade tore through the roof of the car, narrowly missing Grandpa's head. The old man rolled on to his left side, moments before the blade stabbed back up through the space where he'd just been.

The sword sliced up a third time, forcing Grandpa to roll all the way off the roof. He hung on with one hand, the metal toes of his boots scraping along the ground, sending showers of sparks up behind the car.

'Grandpa!' cried Gwen, who was watching the scene from inside The Rust Bucket. Spurred on by the sound of his granddaughter's voice, Grandpa Max began dragging himself back up on to the roof of the speeding car.

Suddenly, a tall dark figure swung in through The Rust Bucket's open door. Gwen screamed at the sight of the Forever Knight, then ducked under his arm as he made a grab at her.

'You want a fight?' Ben bellowed from the front of the vehicle. 'Try picking on someone your own size!'

The knight drew his blazing blue sword and lunged at him, but the boy rolled out of attacking range. Spinning round, the masked villain raised the sword a second time and advanced. Ben glanced down at the Omnitrix. Still red. Still useless. There was no escaping this time. He was done for!

THWACK! The door of the motorhome's small fridge flew open, smacking the knight in the face. He staggered backwards towards the motorhome's side door, stunned by the blow. Ben glanced up at his cousin, who stood next to the fridge, giving him a thumbs-up.

Acting quickly, Ben snatched up a cast-iron cooking pot. It still contained half the meal Grandpa had made for them earlier. Ben grinned. Time to get rid of two problems at once!

Twirling his arm round, Ben launched the pot at the knight. It hit him like a cannonball to the chest. His arms waving about wildly, the villain toppled backwards through the door, where he bounced hard on the hot tarmac road.

'Nice job!' cried Ben and Gwen, giving each other a high five. Their celebrations didn't last long, however. With a splintering crash, the motorhome's sunroof exploded inwards. Through the hole they could make out the shape of the second knight.

Snatching up the fire extinguisher, Gwen rushed over to the shattered sunroof. She pointed the nozzle up through the gap in the ceiling and let rip with the chemical spray.

The cloud of choking gas seeped

in through the gaps in the knight's mask, blinding him and choking him at the same time. Coughing and spluttering, he stepped backwards and slipped off the roof. Screaming, he tumbled all the way off the road bridge they were travelling across, hitting the water below with a distant **SPLASH**.

Grandpa Max was back on the roof of Enoch's car, but he didn't know how long for. The blade of the sword had turned the metal into something resembling Swiss cheese, and still Enoch continued to stab at him.

An idea struck him. As the blue blade swished up at him for what felt like the fiftieth time, Grandpa attached one of the magnetic pads to it. The pad wedged against the roof, making it impossible for Enoch to pull the sword back through.

Inside the car, Enoch growled. He pulled with all his strength, but the sword was well and truly stuck. The knight glanced down at the seat next to him. At least he still had . . .

The mask! Where was the mask? Enoch stood up and stuck his head out through the sunroof. Over in The Rust Bucket doorway, Grandpa Max held up the Mask of Ah Puch. He gave Enoch a wink, then stepped inside, pulling the door shut behind him.

Relieved to have the mask back, Grandpa clambered back into the driver's seat of his beloved motorhome. His blood ran cold when he looked out through the front window; an enormous truck was heading straight towards them!

Grandpa tried to swerve, but Enoch's car blocked The Rust Bucket's escape. The truck was close, and getting closer by the second. Soon, there would be no escape. Any second now, they were going to crash!

CHAPTER FOUR

THE TEMPLE OF EK CHUAH

'**H**old on!' Grandpa barked. He pressed another button and yet more jet engines unfolded from within The Rust Bucket. The motorhome sped up rapidly, rocketing towards the oncoming truck.

The rocket boosters took it soaring past Enoch's car. Grandpa twisted the steering hard to the right. The sudden turn forced The Rust Bucket up on to just three of its six wheels. The truck blared its horn as it thundered past, just centimetres from the teetering motorhome.

When they were safely past the eighteen-wheeler, Grandpa Max wrenched the wheel again, bringing The Rust Bucket back down on to all six wheels. A stunned Enoch could only watch as a hatch opened in the back of the speeding motorhome, and hundreds of spiky metal balls spilled out on to the road.

BANG! BANG! BANG! BANG! The tyres on Enoch's car burst instantly and the vehicle skidded to a clumsy stop in the middle of the road. The knight punched a number into his mobile phone as he watched the motorhome flee. The phone rang twice before it was answered.

'Send in the bird,' hissed Enoch.

❈ ❈ ❈

A few miles further along the road, a bright-red warning light blinked on the dashboard of The Rust Bucket. With a cough and a wheeze, the turbo boosters shuddered to a stop. The motorhome slowed gradually before coming to a halt, clouds of steam rising from the overheated engine.

Grandpa dug his toolbox out from under the driver's seat, stomped outside and began the job of figuring out what had caused the engine to fail.

Gwen and Ben stepped down behind him, Ben clutching the Mask of Ah Puch in his hands. He turned it over, studying the gruesome-looking object. It didn't *look* all that special – just creepy, really.

As the eyes of the mask caught the sun's rays, they began to glow a bright green. Ben gulped nervously as twin beams of emerald light projected from the eye sockets and down on to the dusty ground.

'Uh . . . Grandpa?'

'Not now, Ben,' snapped his grandfather, still busy tinkering with the engine.

'I think you're gonna want to see this,' Ben insisted.

Sighing, Grandpa Max turned to his grandson. He gasped at what he saw. The mask was projecting a holographic image of an ancient Mayan temple. It looked almost real enough to touch.

'It's the map to the ancient Mayan temple of Ek Chuah,' said Grandpa. A horrible thought suddenly struck him. If Ben had been able to find the map so easily, then that meant Enoch probably had too!

Grandpa dropped his tools. There was no time to lose. He looked at Ben and nodded towards the Omnitrix. 'We need to beat them to that temple!'

✖ ✖ ✖

Stinkfly buzzed low over an ancient South American jungle, struggling to stay in the air. It had taken a long time to fly this far, mostly because he'd had to carry Grandpa and Gwen the whole way. Gwen he could manage, but Grandpa really could do with losing some weight!

'Can't you go any faster?' his grandfather demanded.

'I'm sorry, Grandpa,' Stinkfly replied. 'I'm not used to flying with passengers.'

His four alien eyes squinted. Up ahead, he could make out the top of the temple. They were getting close. Just as well, because the Omnitrix had started to flash, and any moment now they would all –

They screamed as they fell. High, twisting branches clawed at them, slowing them down, saving them from becoming pancakes on the jungle floor. With a **THUD! THUD! THUD!** all three of them hit the ground. Ben spat out a mouthful of leaves he'd collected on the way down.

'Man –' he winced –'I really need to work on my emergency landings.'

Grandpa Max paused in the foliage near the temple. A black helicopter stood silently next to the ancient ruins. The Forever Knights were already here. Peering through the trees, he could see the villains. They were trying to blow open the temple doors with dynamite, but weren't having any luck.

Keeping low, Grandpa led Gwen and Ben up towards the far side of the temple. He studied the wall. Its giant bricks had been carved from solid rock. There was no way they could break through.

'There's always a secret entrance to these temples,' Grandpa Max muttered. He pushed a few of the stones. 'Where *is* it?'

Ben unclipped the mask from his grandfather's belt. He held it up over his face and peered through the eyeholes.

'Ben, what are you doing?' Grandpa demanded.

'If this thing could show us how to get this far, maybe it can show us how to get in.'

Ben slowly turned his gaze across the wall. Aside from everything having a faint green tint, it all looked pretty much normal.

Wait! He backtracked along the bricks. One of the stone blocks seemed to be giving off a faint yellow glow. Ben stepped forwards and touched the brick. At once, a hidden doorway slid open before him, and Ben, Gwen and Grandpa Max stepped inside.

The temple smelled of damp and death. The faint glow from the sun outside was the only source of light as they hurried along a narrow stone corridor.

'The sword would be kept in the centre of the temple, on the lowest floor,' Grandpa announced. 'There should be some stairs nearby.'

'Stairs?' Ben winced. 'Where's the express elevator when you really need it?'

The darkness enveloped them now, making it impossible to see. Grandpa felt along the wall for a torch. When he found one, he lit it using a spark from a fire-lighting device on his Plumber suit. The torch burst into a bright-orange ball of flame in his hand.

Ben looked down and realised his toes were poking over the edge of an enormous drop. Shocked, he lost his balance and began to topple forward. He span his arms in wide circles, desperately trying to straighten up, but it was no use. He was going to fall!

A strong hand caught him by the belt of his trousers. Ben breathed a sigh of relief when Grandpa heaved him back up to safety.

'Whew, that was close,' breathed Grandpa Max. 'Almost lost the mask!'

'OK,' whispered Gwen as their grandfather set off towards the stairs. 'Would you say obsessed?'

Ben nodded. 'Once he gets that sword, he'll be himself again, right?'

Gwen could only shrug. The way Grandpa was acting, there was no saying if he'd ever be himself again.

✖ ✖ ✖

Ben wheezed as they finally arrived at one of the lower levels of the temple. Grandpa was already there, studying a carved stone that stood in the middle of the room. The indent on top of it looked to be a perfect match for the Mask of Ah Puch.

'This is it,' said Grandpa Max. He held the mask above the stone. Finally, after all these years, he would –

'Who says you can't get a Plumber when you need one?' cackled Enoch, as he stepped from the shadows. Two Forever Knights raced forward and snatched Ben and Gwen. They struggled, but the knights were too strong. 'Without you bringing the mask,' continued Enoch, 'we wouldn't have been able to get inside the great chamber.'

Grandpa felt like crying out. How could he have been so stupid? Whatever happened next would be all his fault!

He was too consumed by guilt to notice Enoch prise the mask from his fingers. The leader of the knights spent a few seconds admiring the prize he had worked so hard to win.

Enoch walked slowly across to the other side of the room and stopped by a wide circular hole in the ground. The Forever Knights dragged Ben and Gwen behind him, leaving Grandpa Max with no choice but to follow.

'Legend has it that The Eternal Pit of Despair is bottomless,' he said. He caught hold of Ben with one hand and dragged him closer to the edge. He grinned wickedly beneath his mask. 'Let's find out!'

With a sudden jerk of his arm, Enoch hurled Ben into the The Eternal Pit of Despair. Screaming in terror, Ben plunged helplessly down into the darkness.

THE ALIEN VS THE DEATH GOD

Ben felt his stomach do a flip as he tumbled down the hole. Panicked, he slammed his hand down on the Omnitrix, not sure which alien he had chosen, but certain they all had more chance of surviving than he did.

In a flash of green light, he became the mighty Four Arms. Lucky break. Maybe he'd get out of this yet!

Gritting his teeth, Four Arms dug every one of his fingers deep into the wall of the pit. His powerful grip splintered the rock as he gradually slowed himself down.

After several long seconds, he came to a complete stop. Now all he had to do was climb back out! Steeling himself, he looked up, only to see Gwen and Grandpa plummeting towards him.

Anchoring himself on two hands, Four Arms swang out from the wall. His two free hands found their targets, snatching his grand-father and Gwen from the air as they passed.

They all hung there for a moment, catching their breath. It was Gwen who finally broke the silence.

'Next summer,' she whimpered, 'I am so going to band camp!'

Enoch and a squad of his Forever Knights stood in the chamber of Ek Chuah. They had used the mask to open the doors, and now before them stood a scale model of the temple – a giant, pyramid-like structure, thirty metres high. Right at the very top of the construction, the Sword of Ek Chuah stood silent and still.

'Magnificent,' hissed Enoch. 'Bring it to me!'

The knights nodded and stepped further into the chamber. As they did, a low, rumbling growl echoed from all directions. The villains raised their weapons. Whatever was in there with them didn't sound happy!

✖ ✖ ✖

Four Arms heaved Grandpa out of the pit. The hulking alien clambered up behind him, Gwen clinging tightly to his shoulders.

'Grandpa, I think Gwen needs a second to catch her breath,' he said.

Halfway towards the open chamber doors, Grandpa spun round. 'No can do,' he snapped. 'Enoch may already have the sword.'

'Ever since the alarm went off, that sword is all you think about!'

'You two have to keep your eyes on the prize and remember what's important here!'

'We do remember,' Four Arms replied. 'Do you?'

Before Grandpa could answer, a Forever Knight crashed into the wall next to him. An inhuman howl boomed from within the next chamber, and Grandpa Max rushed over to look.

Slipping from Four Arms' shoulders, Gwen crept after Grandpa, followed close behind by her big red cousin.

Inside the chamber, some kind of giant monster was tossing the other knights around like they were rag dolls. When it spotted the newcomers, the creature screeched with rage.

'It must be Ah Puch,' Grandpa whispered. 'The Mayan God of Death and the Underworld. He's the guardian of the Sword of Ek Chuah.'

'Why can't places like this ever be protected by, like, The Guardian of Cheerfulness?' Gwen groaned. 'Is that too much to ask?'

Ah Puch lifted a struggling Forever Knight into the air, then slammed him down on to a pile of rocks. 'Looks like he's pounding the bad guys for us,' said Four Arms with a shrug.

'Ben, keep him occupied while we get the sword,' instructed Grandpa, creeping over to the stairs that led to the top of the miniature monument.

'Yo, Rat Puke!' the alien bellowed. Ah Puch spun, his red eyes blazing hatred. Four Arms clenched his fists and snarled, 'Come get some!'

Ah Puch covered the distance between them in the blink of an eye. A punch like none he'd ever felt sent Four Arms crashing backwards through a wall. He lashed out with an uppercut, but the monster simply dodged it.

Screeching, Ah Puch brought both fists down on Four Arms, driving the alien down into the rock floor. Again and again the God of Death pummelled his helpless foe, each blow harder and more savage than the one before.

Up on the monument, Grandpa fired a mini grappling hook from the arm of his

Plumber suit. He caught the sword with his first shot, but a bright-blue blade immediately sliced through the rope.

Grandpa Max ducked under a Forever Knight's attack, then stood up quickly, throwing the villain over his shoulder and back down the crumbling stone steps.

Grandpa quickly continued to clamber up towards the sword. Even from this distance, he could feel its power. He had to get to it before Enoch. He *had* to!

Less than a metre from the weapon, he heard Gwen scream his name. He spun round, only to find her some way down the stairs, about to be cut in half by another of the Forever Knights.

Grandpa glanced at the sword. It was the key to either destroying the world, or to saving it. He gritted his teeth. It would have to wait.

Stamping his foot, Grandpa Max kicked the hidden rocket boosters in his boots into action. A burst of flame sent him flying down the steps. He hit the knight like a human battering ram, sending him crashing back down the stairs.

In the corner of the chamber, Four Arms crunched two powerful right hooks into Ah Puch's jaw. The creature howled and flicked out his long, pointed tongue. It wrapped round the alien like a giant snake. With a sudden twist of his misshapen head, Ah Puch whipped Four Arms into the air. The hero barely had time to brace for impact before he was slammed back down against the rocky floor.

Through swollen eyes, Four Arms peered up at the Sword of Ek Chuah. Grandpa and Gwen had made it up there – but so had Enoch! The knight was swinging wildly with his energy sword. Grandpa and Gwen were managing to avoid the attacks, but they couldn't dodge forever.

'No!' gasped the alien as Enoch spun to face Grandpa. His sword was raised, ready to deliver one final, fatal strike.

Four Arms moved his four fists upwards as one, focusing all his strength into a single, devastating blow.

BOOM! The cavern itself seemed to shake when the punch connected with Ah Puch's jaw. The force of the strike sent the monster flipping backwards. Ah Puch squealed in pain as he slammed against the side of the model temple.

The pyramid shuddered, causing Grandpa and Gwen to slide off the top. They landed next to the motionless body of Ah Puch, just as the Ominitrix gave a red flash.

Ben looked down at his human form. 'Ah, not good!'

Grandpa was already powering back up the monument, desperately trying to reach the sword before Enoch could seize it. But the sudden screams of his grandchildren made him stop.

Ah Puch was back on his feet, and advancing towards Ben and Gwen. Without any aliens to call on, they were surely doomed. But the sword! If Enoch got his hands on it, then everyone was doomed. It was the easiest decision Grandpa had ever made.

'Why don't you go back to the barn, birdbrain?' he bellowed, hurling himself on to Ah Puch's back.

Ben and Gwen raced round behind the monster. Together, they slammed their shoulders against the backs of Ah Puch's knees, just as Grandpa leaped clear. Thrown off balance, the death god tumbled all the way to the bottom of the steps. This time he didn't get back up.

The heroes spun, ready to race to the top of the pyramid. They gasped as they realised they were too late. Enoch already had the sword! He cackled as he held the blade aloft.

'At last! The ultimate weapon!' he crowed. 'The world shall kneel before . . .'

He let the rest of the sentence tail off, as the sword crumbled to dust in his hands.

Down below, Grandpa Max blinked, then let rip with a belly laugh of his own. 'I guess that's what happens when your ultimate weapon is five thousand years old,' he chuckled.

Suddenly, the walls of the temple began to shake. Large chunks of rock broke from the roof and smashed against the floor of the chamber. The sword must have been booby trapped. It was time to go!

Panting and wheezing, the Tennysons tumbled through the secret door of the temple. Behind them, the ancient construction collapsed in on itself, trapping Enoch and his knights inside.

'Well,' said Grandpa Max with a grin, wiping the dust from his Plumber suit, 'I could sure go for some dung-beetle stew. It's even better reheated, you know?'

Gwen and Ben looked at each other

and smiled. His jokes might be awful, and his cooking might stink, but it sure was nice to have the old Grandpa back!

HAVE YOU SEEN THEM ALL?

Ben 10 colour storybook 1 **(And Then There Were 10/The Krakken)**	978 1 4052 4165 6	£3.99
Ben 10 colour storybook 2 **(Permanent Retirement/Side Effects)**	978 1 4052 4166 3	£3.99
Ben 10 Annual 2009	978 1 4052 3909 7	£6.99
Ben 10 Scratch and Show Activity Book	978 1 4052 3887 8	£3.99

Ben 10 Sticker Action	978 1 4052 3881 6	£3.99
Ben 10 Alien Hero Handbook	978 1 4052 3886 1	£4.99
Ben 10 Touch Screen Activity Book	978 1 4052 4523 4	£4.99
Ben 10 chapter storybook 1 **(And Then There Were 10/Kevin 11)**	978 1 4052 4467 1	£3.99
Ben 10 chapter storybook 2 **(The Alliance/Secrets)**	978 1 4052 4468 8	£3.99

COMING SOON ...
2 COOL BEN 10 COMIC STRIP BOOKS!

And Then There Were 10   978 1 4052 4663 7   £4.99

Washington B.C.   978 1 4052 4664 4   £4.99

AVAILABLE FROM ALL
GOOD BOOKSHOPS
OR ORDER DIRECT FROM
WWW.EGMONT.CO.UK